Meet the Author
www.darylcobb.com

Meet the Illustrator
www.abigaildaker.com

Printed in the USA
Published by 10 To 2 Children's Books

MW01134268

I children jor at writing ... ... inspiring and, combined with his love for music and the guitar, he discovered a passion for songwriting. This talent would motivate him for years to come and the rhythm he created with his music also found its way into the bedtime stories he later created for his children. The story "Boy on the Hill," about a boy who turns the clouds into animals, was his first bedtime story/song and was inspired by his son and an infatuation with the shapes of clouds. Through the years his son and daughter have inspired so much of his work, including "Daniel Dinosaur" and "Daddy Did I Ever Say? I Love You, Love You, Every Day."

Daryl spends a lot of his time these days visiting schools promoting literacy with his interactive educational assemblies "Teaching Through Creative Arts: A Writer's Journey." These performance programs teach children about the writing and creative process and allow Daryl to do what he feels is most important -- inspire children to read and write. He also performs at benefits and libraries with his "Music & Storytime" shows.

Other books by Daryl K. Cobb:

"Do Pirates Go To School?"
"Pirates: Legend of the Snarlyfeet"
"Bill the Bat Baby Sits Bella"
"Bill the Bat Finds His Way Home"
"Bill the Bat Loves Halloween"
"Barnyard Buddies: Perry Parrot Finds a Purpose"
"Daddy Did I Ever Say? I Love You,
  Love You, Every Day"
"Daniel Dinosaur"
"Count With Daniel Dinosaur"
"Henry Hare's Floppy Socks"

Find all of Daryl's books at www.darylcobb.com

Boy on the Hill

Written by Daryl K. Cobb

Illustrated by Abigail Daker

ISBN 9781453793800

Written by Daryl K. Cobb
Illustrated by Abigail Daker

10 To 2 Children's Books

Time to Read ™

I dedicate this
book to my son Cameron.
He has inspired many stories
over the years,
but this one is so very special,
because it was the first.

Daryl K. Cobb

To Joseph and Stu.

Abigail Daker

Once upon a time
there was a little boy.

He lived **high** on a hill,
   oh, what a joy!

He'd reach his hands in the air and
twirl the clouds around.

He'd turn them into funny things,
he'd turn them into clowns.

He'd turn them into puppy dogs
that chase around their tails.

He'd turn them into kitty cats
playing with a pail.

He'd turn them into little birds
that sing a **happy** tune.

He could turn them into anything.
He could turn one into you.

He'd swirl them with his left hand
and twirl them with his right.

He'd even use his feet
to make the clouds come out right.

He'd make a butterfly
and a little bumblebee.

He even made a squirrel
climbing a tree.

He'd make them into **anything** and **everything** he could.

He made a chubby beaver
gnawing on wood.

He made a little lion cub
and his friend the bear.

He made a bunny rabbit
and her cousin the hare.

So now you won't think it's strange
to see a **floating** cow.

A duck,

a chick,

a pig,

Let me say it, I'll say it again...

Once upon a time
    there was a little boy.

He lived **high** on a hill,
oh, what a *joy!*

Made in the USA
Charleston, SC
13 November 2012